AMONG US COLORING BOOK FOR KIDS AND ADULTS

Coloring Hilarious and Relaxing Scenes From 2020's Breakout Game

CREWMEMBER PUBLICATIONS

Welcome to This Epic Coloring Adventure!

Are you ready to catch the imposter?

Among Us is a multiplayer game where players are dropped onto an alien spaceship. Each player is designated a private role as a "crewmate" or "impostor." Crewmates must run around the ship and try to complete a set of tasks while trying to root out and avoid getting killed by the impostor.

I present to you **Among Us Coloring Book for Kids and Adults: Coloring Hilarious and Relaxing Scenes From 2020's Breakout Game** like no other. Color these hilarious illustrations of Among Us game characters that will surely give you fun and relaxation after a long and tiring day. If you love playing Among Us, you'll definitely love the following coloring pages! So, turn the page now, and color these funny scenes while catching the mighty imposter!

AMONG US

A1
A2
A3
A4
B2
B3
B4
NR
C3
C4

TMNT

BOB WAS NOT AN IMPOSTOR.

TED WAS AN IMPOSTOR.

AILY PLANE

!
DUM

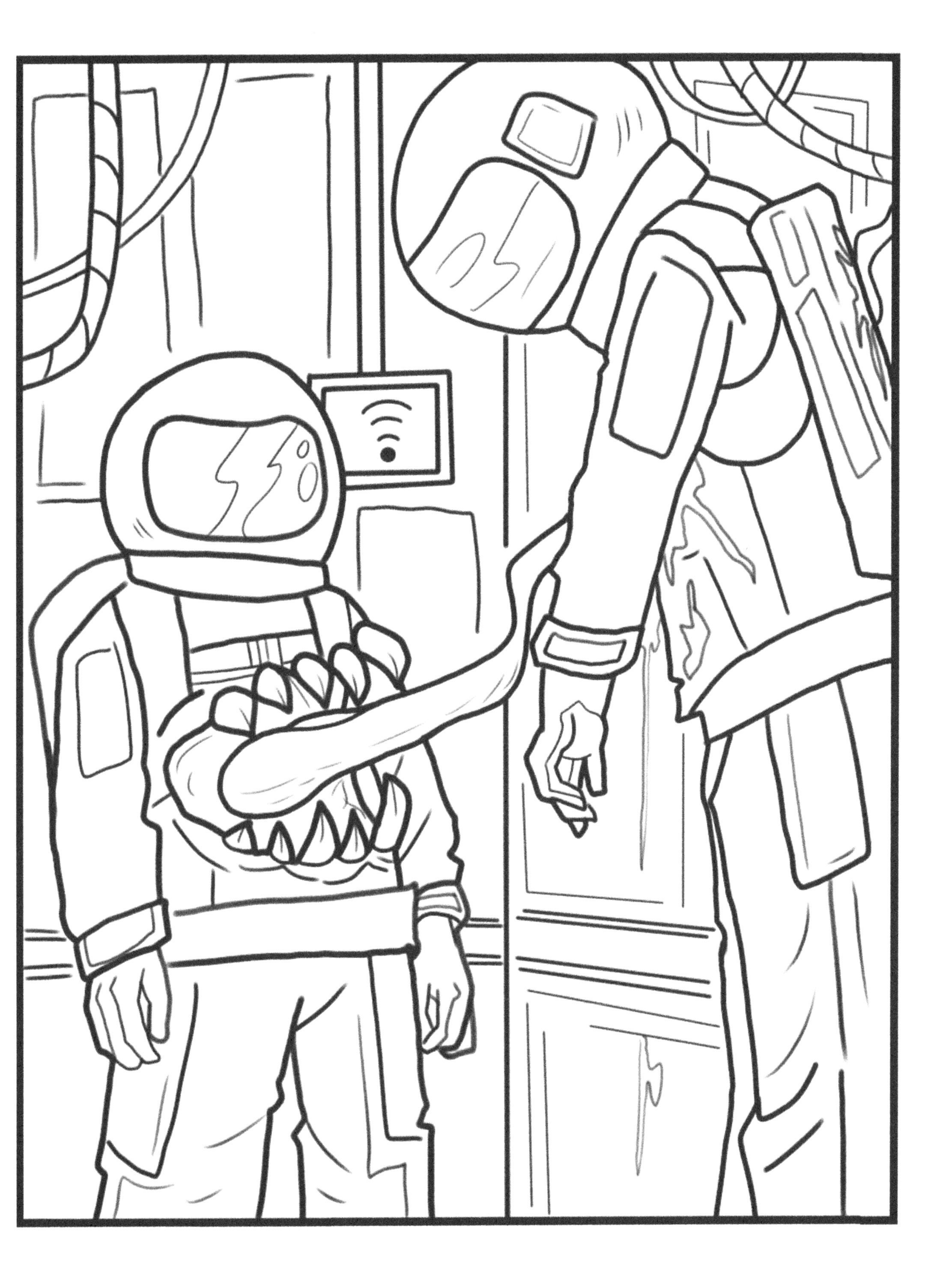

DON'T FORGET TO LEAVE AN AMAZON REVIEW!

Were you able to find the imposters? We hope you've enjoyed bringing these hilarious scenes and game characters to life through your coloring. **Among Us Coloring Book Kids and Adults: Coloring Hilarious and Relaxing Scenes From 2020's Breakout Game** was created to bring fun and relaxation to Among Us players, inspiring artists, and anyone who simply loves to color and have fun!

If you liked this book, then we'd appreciate you letting us know through an honest review in the Amazon product page. Reviews are the lifeblood of our publishing endeavors. A 5-star review would mean the world to us. We're counting with yours!

Thank you for choosing Crewmember Publications.

Made in the USA
Monee, IL
27 November 2020